The Giant Jelly Bean Jar

by **Marcie Aboff**
pictures by **Paige Billin-Frye**

DUTTON CHILDREN'S BOOKS
New York

jE

For my mother, with much love always—M.A.
For Emily and Bob—P.B.

Text copyright © 2004 by Marcie Aboff
Illustrations copyright © 2004 by Paige Billin-Frye

CIP Data is available.

Published in the United States of America by Dutton Children's Books,
a division of Penguin Young Readers Group
345 Hudson Street, New York, New York 10014
www.penguin.com

Manufactured in China
First Edition
1 3 5 7 9 10 8 6 4 2
ISBN 0-525-47236-3

Ben loved jelly beans.

He loved going

to Jo-Jo's Jelly Bean Shop.

Every weekend Jo-Jo had a contest.

Jo-Jo read a riddle and said,

"Guess which jelly bean flavor

is the answer to my riddle."

The person with the right answer

won a jar full of jelly beans.

Every Saturday, Ben went

to Jo-Jo's shop with his sister, Jill.

"Yum," Ben said.

"Today I am going to win that jar."

"You say that every week," Jill said.

It was hard to win the prize.

You had to say the answer

in a loud voice.

You had to say it

in front of everyone in the store!

Ben always knew the answers

to Jo-Jo's riddles.

But he never won the jelly beans.

"You are too shy," Jill said every week.
She told him to raise his hand high
and to speak up.
"Okay," said Ben quietly.

Inside Jo-Jo's shop,

Ben and Jill passed jars and jars

full of jelly beans.

There were apple jelly beans,

bubble gum jelly beans,

and grape jam jelly beans.

There were even popcorn jelly beans!

Jo-Jo stepped out from behind the counter.

"Hello, my friends!"

he called out.

The kids cheered.

"Here is this week's

jelly bean riddle," Jo-Jo said.

"I'm a long, yellow fruit
With skin you peel back.
I'm tasty with breakfast
And I make a great snack!"

Kids waved their hands high in the air.

Ben saw Jill raise her hand.

He raised his hand, too.

But he was very nervous.

He saw bigger kids. He heard louder kids.

Ben lowered his hand.

Jo-Jo looked at the children.

He pointed to Jill.

"Banana!" Jill cried.

"You are right!" Jo-Jo said.

"We have a jelly bean princess!"

"Oh, nuts!" Ben said to himself.

"I knew the answer, too!"

"Here, Ben," Jill said.

She gave him some jelly beans.

"I'll share my prize with you."

Ben did not say anything.

He wanted to answer

the jelly bean riddle himself.

The next Saturday, Ben and Jill
went back to Jo-Jo's shop.
"Who is ready to be
this week's winner?" Jo-Jo asked.
Everyone cheered.

"Guess this jelly bean flavor,"

Jo-Jo said.

"I am a big round pie

With cheese and sauce, too.

A slice would be nice—

How many for you?"

Jill whispered, "Go for it, Ben!"

Ben raised his hand.

This time, he did not lower it.

But there was another boy

whose hand was higher.

Jo-Jo pointed to that boy instead of Ben.

"Pizza!" the boy shouted.

"Right!" Jo-Jo said.

"Here is a jelly bean jar

for my new jelly bean prince."

"Oh, nuts!" Ben said to himself.

"Not again!"

Ben and Jill walked home together.

"Don't worry, Ben," Jill said.

"Next time you'll win for sure."

The next Saturday, Ben and Jill

went to Jo-Jo's shop again.

But this week was different.

It was special.

Jo-Jo's Jelly Bean Shop had been open

for one year.

Jo-Jo was having a big party.

The store was more crowded than ever.

Jo-Jo stepped out from behind the counter.

He raised a very, very big jar

of jelly beans over his head.

Everyone cheered.

"Who will be my Grand Prize
winner today?" he asked.
Kids waved their hands high.
"Me, me!" they called out.

Ben just looked at the jelly bean jar.

It was the biggest jar

he had ever seen!

He listened carefully to Jo-Jo's riddle.

"I'm yummy with jelly

And can be spooned from a jar.

Between slices of bread

I'm a true sandwich star!"

Ben knew the answer right away.

This time, he lifted his hand high.

Then he looked at the jar again.

He raised his hand a little higher.

Then he raised it as high as he could.

He even stood on his tippy-toes!

Jo-Jo looked out at the big crowd.

He pointed to Ben.

Ben was so surprised,

he forgot the answer

to the riddle!

Everyone waited for Ben to speak.

But he didn't say anything.

Some people started to wave

their hands again.

"Me, me!" they shouted.

Ben still did not say anything.

Jill looked at the crowd.

Then she looked at Ben.

She lifted up her foot.

She stepped right on Ben's toes.

"OH, NUTS!" Ben cried out.

Nuts, Ben thought.

"Peanuts," he whispered.

Then Ben remembered

the answer to the riddle.

In a big voice, he yelled,

28

"Yes!" Jill shouted.

"Yes!" Jo-Jo cried.

Jo-Jo placed a sparkling crown

on Ben's head.

He handed Ben the great

big jelly bean prize jar.

"How does it feel to be
the Grand Prize Jelly Bean King?"
Jill asked Ben.

"Great!" Ben said, loud and clear.

He did not feel one bit nervous.

On the way home,

Jill patted Ben on the back.

"You did it!" she said.

Ben grinned.

"Thank you for stepping

on my toes!" he said.

Jill grinned back.

"That's what sisters are for!"